SPOTLIGHT ON CIVIC ACTION

# CONSTITUTIONAL DEMOCRACY

ELISE COLLIER

**PowerKiDS** *press*

NEW YORK

Published in 2018 by The Rosen Publishing Group, Inc.
29 East 21st Street, New York, NY 10010

Copyright © 2018 by The Rosen Publishing Group, Inc.

All rights reserved. No part of this book may be reproduced in any form without permission in writing from the publisher, except by a reviewer.

Editor: Theresa Morlock
Book Design: Michael Flynn
Interior Layout: Tanya Dellaccio

Photo Credits: Cover Eric Purcell/Moment/Getty Images; p. 5 Sanchai Kumar/Shutterstock.com; pp. 6, 13, 25 Courtesy of OurDocuments.gov; p. 7 MPI/Archive Photos/Getty Images; p. 8 Pool/Getty Images News/Getty Images; p. 9 Michael Kovac/Getty Images Entertainment/Getty Images; p. 11 Scott Olson/Getty Images News/Getty Images; p. 15 UniversalImagesGroup/Getty Images; p. 17 Bettmann/Getty Images; p. 18 Chip Somodevilla/Getty Images News/Getty Images; p 19 https://commons.wikimedia.org/wiki/File:Franklin_Roosevelt_signing_declaration_of_war_against_Germany.jpg; p. 20 Drew Angerer/Getty Images News/Getty Images;
p. 21 Library of Congress/Hulton Archive/Getty Images; p. 22 https://commons.wikimedia.org/wiki/File:Marbury.jpg;
p. 23 Everett - Art/Shutterstock.com; p. 24 Georgios Kollidas/Shutterstock.com; p. 27 https://commons.wikimedia.org/wiki/File:Antoine-Fran%C3%A7ois_Callet_-_Louis_XVI,_roi_de_France_et_de_Navarre_(1754-1793),_rev%C3%AAtu_du_grand_costume_royal_en_1779_-_Google_Art_Project.jpg;
p. 29 FREDERIC J. BROWN/AFP/Getty Images.

Cataloging-in-Publication Data

Names: Collier, Elise.
Title: Constitutional democracy / Elise Collier .
Description: New York : PowerKids Press, 2018. | Series: Spotlight on civic action | Includes index.
Identifiers: ISBN 9781538327913 (pbk.) | ISBN 9781508163961 (library bound) | ISBN 9781538328033 (6 pack)
Subjects: LCSH: Democracy--Juvenile literature. | Constitutional law--United States--Juvenile literature. | State, The--Juvenile literature.
Classification: LCC JC423.C6398 2018 | DDC 321.8--dc23

Manufactured in the United States of America

CPSIA Compliance Information: Batch #BW18PK For further information contact Rosen Publishing, New York, New York at 1-800-237-9932.

# CONTENTS

OUR AMERICAN GOVERNMENT . . . . . . . . . . . . . . . . . . . . . . . .4
WE THE PEOPLE. . . . . . . . . . . . . . . . . . . . . . . . . . . . . . . . . . . .6
REPRESENTATION . . . . . . . . . . . . . . . . . . . . . . . . . . . . . . . . . .8
MAJORITY RULE, MINORITY RIGHTS . . . . . . . . . . . . . . . . . .10
THE CONSTITUTION . . . . . . . . . . . . . . . . . . . . . . . . . . . . . . .12
FEDERAL AND STATE POWERS. . . . . . . . . . . . . . . . . . . . . . .14
SEPARATION OF POWERS . . . . . . . . . . . . . . . . . . . . . . . . . . .16
THE LEGISLATIVE BRANCH . . . . . . . . . . . . . . . . . . . . . . . . .18
THE EXECUTIVE BRANCH . . . . . . . . . . . . . . . . . . . . . . . . . . .20
THE JUDICIAL BRANCH . . . . . . . . . . . . . . . . . . . . . . . . . . . .22
THE ROOTS OF DEMOCRACY . . . . . . . . . . . . . . . . . . . . . . . .24
THE AGE OF ENLIGHTENMENT . . . . . . . . . . . . . . . . . . . . . .26
A SOCIAL CONTRACT . . . . . . . . . . . . . . . . . . . . . . . . . . . . . .28
LIBERTY AND JUSTICE FOR ALL . . . . . . . . . . . . . . . . . . . . .30
GLOSSARY . . . . . . . . . . . . . . . . . . . . . . . . . . . . . . . . . . . . . . .31
INDEX. . . . . . . . . . . . . . . . . . . . . . . . . . . . . . . . . . . . . . . . . . .32
PRIMARY SOURCE LIST . . . . . . . . . . . . . . . . . . . . . . . . . . . .32
WEBSITES . . . . . . . . . . . . . . . . . . . . . . . . . . . . . . . . . . . . . . .32

CHAPTER ONE

# OUR AMERICAN GOVERNMENT

The United States is a republic. That means the people elect representatives who run the government. It is also a democracy, which is government elected by the people, directly or indirectly.

The United States has a constitutional democracy. This is a system in which the government's authority is clearly defined and limited by a constitution. The constitution and other regulations have been put in place to check the government's power and protect the people. The founding principle of our constitutional democracy is popular sovereignty. This means that the government **derives** its authority from the people.

Our constitutional democracy was created to uphold the main values of our nation, including the **inalienable** rights of the people, freedom of expression, the right to privacy, and entitlement to justice and legal and economic equality.

Other countries that currently have constitutional democracies include Germany, Israel, and Japan.

CHAPTER TWO

# WE THE PEOPLE

The U.S. Constitution begins with the words "We the people." The Founding Fathers wanted to create a system of government to serve the many U.S. citizens rather than the few people in power. When the original colonies were under British rule, the American people were subject to the authority of a king with

The original Constitution is on display at the National Archives Building in Washington, D.C.

U.S. CONSTITUTION

This painting shows the signing of the U.S. Constitution in 1787. When the Constitution was created, the men pictured above represented "the people" of America.

no Americans to represent their needs in the British government. When they won their independence, they wanted to make sure they created a system in which the government served the people instead of the people serving the government.

In order to protect the needs of the people, the Founding Fathers created a system of government in which the people would elect officials to represent them. These elected officials would only be allowed to hold their positions for a certain amount of time.

CHAPTER THREE

# REPRESENTATION

In a constitutional democracy, officials are elected to speak for their constituents. A constituent is a voting member of a community. Constituents vote to select representatives to speak for them at the local, state, and federal levels. Mayors are local representatives, state legislators are state representatives, and the president

President Barack Obama was the first African American president in United States history.

Ruth Bader Ginsburg overcame gender-based **discrimination** to become the second woman appointed to the U.S. Supreme Court.

and members of Congress are federal representatives.

All citizens are not equally represented. A minority group is a group of people who are different from the larger group in their country in some way. Some examples of minority groups in the United States include African Americans, Hispanic and Latino Americans, and gay and lesbian Americans. A majority group is a group with the greatest number of people. In a constitutional democracy, it's important to balance majority rule with protecting the rights of minority groups.

## CHAPTER FOUR

# MAJORITY RULE, MINORITY RIGHTS

Majority rule is the idea that the majority has the power to make decisions for everyone. The side with the greatest number of votes has greater influence on elections, passes more bills in Congress, and makes other important government decisions. Majority rule is the basis of a constitutional democracy because it means that the government operates based on the decisions supported by the greatest amount of people.

In principle, majority rule is the fairest way of making decisions. However, majority rule becomes a problem when the majority makes decisions that cause the minority to suffer. This situation is sometimes called majority **tyranny**. To prevent the majority from mistreating minorities, the Constitution protects the fundamental rights of individual citizens and the collective rights of minority groups.

This Arab American girl is protesting a travel ban that would prevent people from certain Muslim countries from entering the United States.

11

CHAPTER FIVE

# THE CONSTITUTION

Most of the laws protecting individual citizens are laid out in the Bill of Rights, which is the first 10 **amendments** to the U.S. Constitution. The individual rights of citizens, which protect them from unjust governmental interference, are called civil liberties. Some examples of civil liberties include freedom of expression, freedom of religion, and the right to **due process**.

The Constitution provides the framework for how our constitutional democracy operates. It is a living document, which means that it continues to change as the nation and its people change. The Constitution provides a stable structure for our government but is open to interpretation. In addition to protecting our civil liberties, the main functions of the Constitution are the division of federal and state powers and the separation of powers of the three branches of the federal government.

BILL OF RIGHTS

The Bill of Rights was ratified in 1791. It made changes to the Constitution to protect the individual rights of citizens.

13

## CHAPTER SIX

# FEDERAL AND STATE POWERS

The Constitution divides authority between the federal and state governments. This system is known as federalism. The federal powers delegated to Congress are called the enumerated powers. The enumerated powers include the power to coin money, impose and collect taxes, borrow money for the United States, regulate interstate business, establish post offices, maintain a navy, and more.

State governments have the power to make and enforce laws, establish courts, collect taxes, build roads, and more. Although the federal government shares some powers with state governments, federal laws are always supreme over state laws. If the federal government considers a state law to be unconstitutional, it has the power to stop that law. These decisions are often made by the U.S. Supreme Court, which interprets federal constitutional law.

Disagreements over states' rights were a key cause of the American Civil War (1861–1865). In the Gettysburg Address, President Abraham Lincoln stressed the importance of preserving the vision of American democracy so the "government of the people, by the people, for the people, shall not perish from the earth."

## CHAPTER SEVEN

# SEPARATION OF POWERS

The Constitution divides the federal government into three branches: the legislative branch, the judicial branch, and the executive branch. Each branch of government has its own powers and responsibilities.

By dividing the federal government into three branches, the Constitution ensures there's a system of checks and balances that regulates government authority. The Founding Fathers felt that creating separation of powers was the only way to avoid the tyranny they had experienced under British rule. In our constitutional democracy, the authority of each federal government branch is limited by the others, meaning that no one branch can become too powerful. For example, the president, who is part of the executive branch, has the power to **veto** laws passed by Congress, which is the legislative branch.

In 1972, President Richard Nixon vetoed a bill called the Comprehensive Child Development Act. The bill would've created universal child care in the United States, but the executive branch used its power to stop it. Nixon opposed the bill because he felt that the government shouldn't take part in helping raise children.

CHAPTER EIGHT

# THE LEGISLATIVE BRANCH

The U.S. Congress forms the legislative branch of the federal government. It is made up of the House of Representatives and the Senate. These bodies are responsible for creating laws.

The House of Representatives has 435 members, one of whom is the Speaker of the House, who leads their proceedings. Each state elects members to the House of Representatives in proportion to the state population.

This photo shows a meeting of Congress in the House Chamber of the U.S. Capitol in Washington, D.C.

The legislative branch is the only branch with the power to declare war. In this photo, President Franklin Delano Roosevelt is shown signing Congress's declaration of war against Germany in 1941.

For example, there are only 2 representatives from Rhode Island in the House of Representatives, but 36 representatives from Texas.

The Senate is made up of 2 senators from each state for a total of 100. Senators hold their positions for a term of 6 years. The vice president of the United States also acts as the president of the Senate.

CHAPTER NINE

# THE EXECUTIVE BRANCH

The president and vice president of the United States are part of the executive branch. The president is elected by the **Electoral College** or by the House of Representatives if no candidate receives a majority of electoral votes. The president is the commander in chief of the armed forces, is responsible for putting Congress's laws into action, and has the power to appoint federal judges.

President Donald Trump won 304 votes from the Electoral College, defeating Hillary Clinton in the 2016 presidential election.

President Andrew Johnson was impeached in 1868. He was the first president to be impeached in U.S. history. This engraving shows Johnson's impeachment trial.

Although you may think of the president as the most powerful person in the country, it's important to remember Congress limits the president's powers. For example, the president needs approval from the Senate to appoint certain federal officials. Congress even has the power to remove the president from office. A president can be impeached, or charged with wrongdoing while in office.

CHAPTER TEN

# THE JUDICIAL BRANCH

The judicial branch is made up of the Supreme Court and other federal courts. The president appoints members of the Supreme Court, who are then voted on by the Senate. Federal Supreme Court judges are appointed for life. Since they don't need to run for reelection or concern themselves with public opinion, they're able to do their job without concern about

In 1803, William Marbury (shown here) began a court case against James Madison (pictured opposite).

The Supreme Court case *Marbury v. Madison* of 1803 established the principle of judicial review.

consequences, although their decisions may be unpopular at the time. Supreme Court justices can, however, be impeached by Congress.

One of the main responsibilities of the Supreme Court is to interpret the Constitution. It does so by making judgments about specific cases and deciding whether or not they're constitutional. The Supreme Court's greatest power is judicial review, which is the power to strike down legislation created by Congress.

CHAPTER ELEVEN

# THE ROOTS OF DEMOCRACY

Our constitutional democracy wasn't created overnight. It was inspired by the ideas of many people and has gone through many changes over time.

An English **philosopher** named John Locke was one of the people whose ideas had the greatest influence in shaping the United States government.

Locke's work *Two Treatises of Government* explores the idea of representative government.

DECLARATION OF INDEPENDENCE

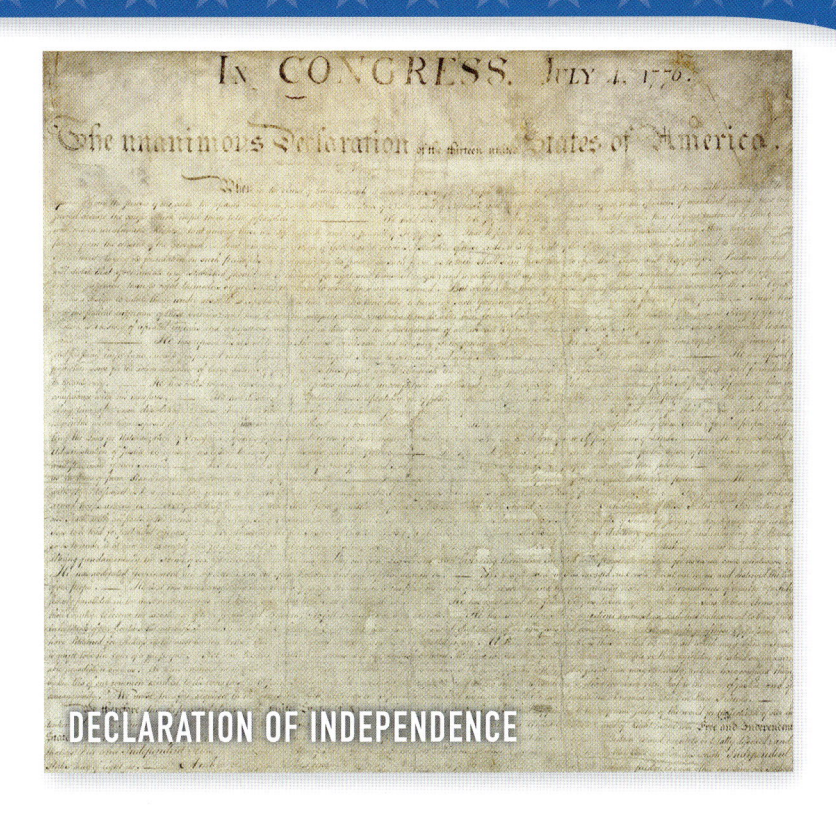

During the 17th century, Locke wrote about government and how it should work. He believed leaders should receive authority to govern from the people and that it was the government's job to protect its peoples' inalienable rights, including life, liberty, and property. He also felt that if the government failed to serve the people, the people had the right to overthrow the government.

Thomas Jefferson was inspired by the writings of John Locke and used his ideas when writing the Declaration of Independence.

CHAPTER TWELVE

# THE AGE OF ENLIGHTENMENT

We owe much of our modern system of government to ideas formed during the Age of Enlightenment, which took place between the late 17th and early 19th centuries. Enlightenment was a movement that highlighted the importance of reason, science, and individual rights. Before the Age of Enlightenment, the dominant form of government was monarchy, in which one ruler has complete authority. During the Enlightenment period, more people began to question and resist the older ideas about how governments and society should be structured.

Enlightenment philosophies like those of John Locke heavily influenced the Founding Fathers when they drafted the Constitution and created their new system of government. The idea that the individual liberties of the people must be respected and protected by their government was inspired by Enlightenment ideas.

Enlightenment philosophies also influenced the French Revolution of 1789 to 1799. The French King Louis XVI (shown here) and his monarchy were overthrown and replaced by a republican government.

## CHAPTER THIRTEEN

# A SOCIAL CONTRACT

Part of John Locke's philosophy about government involved a belief about how governments and their people should interact. This was called the social contract theory. Locke believed the people of a nation sacrifice some of their freedoms with the understanding that the government will protect and serve them.

The social contract theory addresses questions about what responsibilities citizens have to their governments and how governments are responsible for the people. The idea of a social contract between these two parties implies that this relationship is made up of both duties and privileges. As a citizen, you enjoy the privileges of living in a country that has a constitutional democracy. Some of your duties may be required, such as paying taxes and following laws, and others may be voluntary, such as voting and being involved in politics.

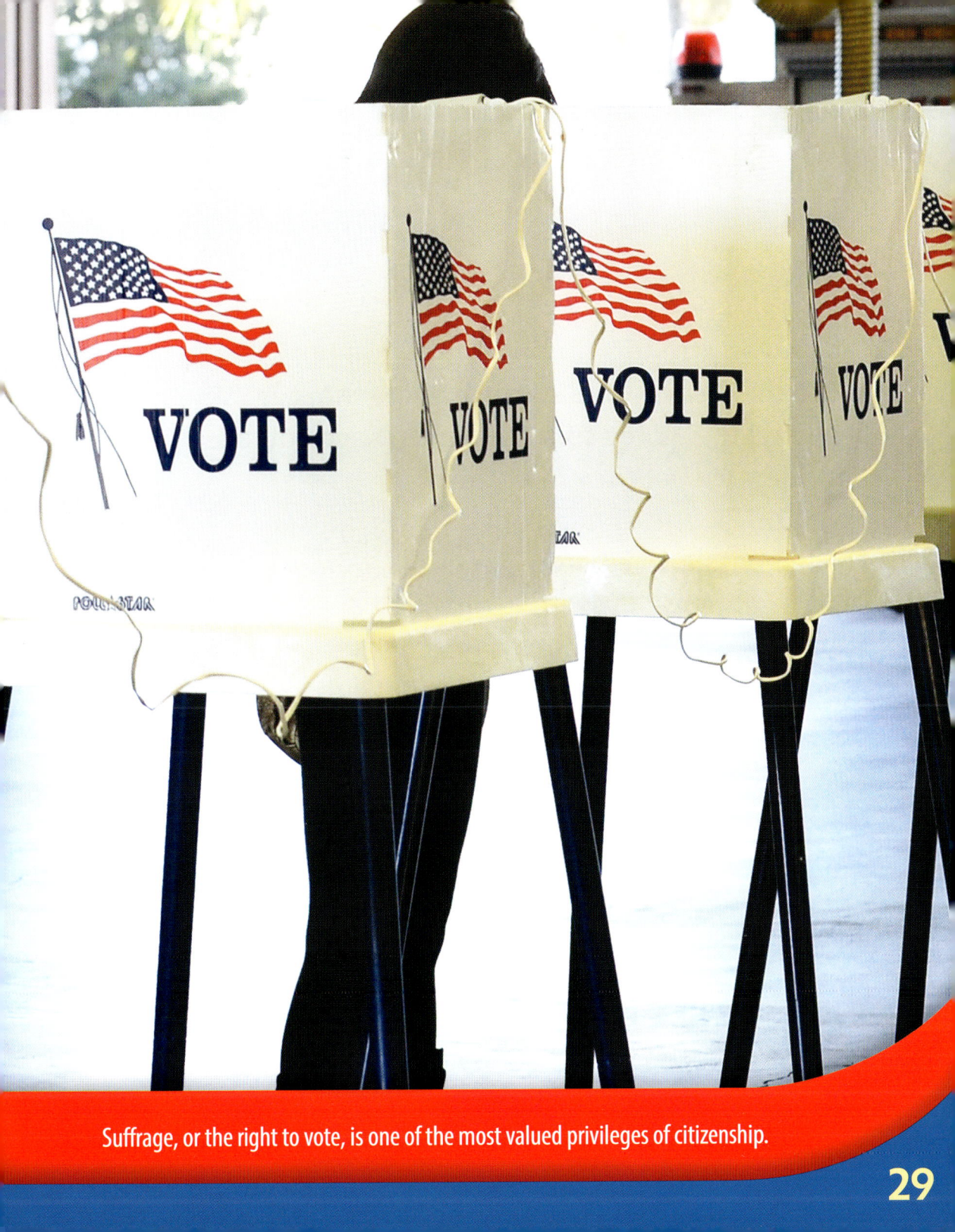

Suffrage, or the right to vote, is one of the most valued privileges of citizenship.

## CHAPTER FOURTEEN

# LIBERTY AND JUSTICE FOR ALL

If you attend a public school, you probably recite the Pledge of Allegiance every morning. Having repeated the words so many times, have you ever considered what they really mean?

The Pledge of Allegiance wraps up the fundamental principles of American democracy in one simple sentence. Citizens promise to be loyal to their country and to the republic, which stands united and promises freedom and fairness to all citizens.

The next time you say the pledge, think carefully about what it means to be part of a constitutional democracy. How has living under this system of government affected your life? Can you identify any parts of it that need to be improved? Most importantly, as a citizen, how can you contribute to improving our constitutional democracy?